5 SCARIER STORIES FOR A DARK KNIGHT

By Matthew Cody

Illustrated by Jeannette Arroyo

Batman created by Bob Kane with Bill Finger

Random House 🏠 New York

Published in the United States by Random House Children's Books, a division of Penguin Random
House LLC, 1745 Broadway, New York, NY 10019, and in Canada by Penguin Random House
Canada Limited, Toronto. Random House and the colophon are registered trademarks of Penguin
Random House LLC.

ISBN 978-0-593-64810-0 (trade) — ISBN 978-0-593-64812-4 (ebook)
Printed in the United States of America

10 9 8 7 6 5 4 3 2 1

Random House Children's Books supports the First Amendment and celebrates the right to read.

CONTENTS

ARKHAM ASYLUM

Ah, welcome to **Arkham**—home to Gotham City's most notorious criminals!

No, no—don't run away. I know I am an unlikely tour guide, but if you think about it, who better to show you around this house of horrors than **The Scarecrow**, the Master of Fear!

And if we hurry it along, we can be finished before sundown. A few of our residents are not the kind of people you want to be alone with after dark. . . .

Anyway, did you know that Arkham is almost two hundred years old? Look at this crumbling plaster and these mildewy walls. They're a fright. Regardless, we also have all the modern security and more. We have cells with bars, heavy doors, and security cameras—look, there's one up there! Smile for the camera now!

This is **the** place to hold the city's most dangerous assortment of criminals, crooks, and **very** bad clowns.

Don't worry, you're not in any **real** danger. I just wanted to see how wide your eyes would get. Fear is so fascinating on a clinical level, don't you think?

But despite the bars and walls and cameras, why do you suppose Gotham City's worst—and I mean the real baddies—don't just break out two minutes after they are locked up?

Why, I'm sure good old Croc would punch a hole in this wall for an extra helping of cornbread during mealtime. And yet escapes are rare.

What keeps them all here . . . hmmm? **FEAR.**

Fear of what? Ah . . . now **that** is
the delicious question. Many would say it's
Batman they are afraid of, but he's only a part of
the puzzle. And the answer is different for everyone. Plus
there are scarier things in Gotham City than Batman.

Take this hallway, for instance—watch your head. If you'll
follow me, I will show you a long, lonely cellblock. Nothing
special about the cells themselves, but the people inside . . .
oh now, that's a tale. Or, rather, **five** tales. You like a good
story, don't you?

Take this poor soul in cell A11B. You see him in there?
Little man staring at . . . what's that he's got on his hand?
A sock puppet?"

Arnold! Put that puppet away! You know the rules.

Arnold Wesker, occupant of cell A11B, is not allowed
puppets of any kind, **no** exceptions. But you probably know
him by his other name—**the Ventriloquist!**

Listen and I'll tell you a story. There's a reason he's
so desperate for company. . . .

ONE

THE HAUNTING
OF LORELEI LEE

Grady's Pawnshop closed at 6:00 pm regularly, six days a week, excluding Sundays. You'd never find Grady's closed at 5:59 pm—just in case he got one last customer. He dreamed of that one special customer who'd wander in and buy more than a few dollars' worth of junk. That one customer who'd spend enough to let Grady take a nice little vacation to Metropolis. Or maybe Coast City.

And Gotham City is so cold this time of year, Grady thought with a small shiver as he reached to turn the OPEN sign to CLOSED.

Of course, you wouldn't find Grady's Pawnshop open at 6:01 pm, either. This was Gotham City, after all, and old Grady did not do business after sundown.

That was why it was so odd on this particular Friday to find the store's "closed" sign hanging in the window at just after 4:00 pm. . . .

"What are ya telling me, Grady? You sayin' dat this cash is all there is?"

Old man Grady could feel the sweat bead along his upper lip. He leaned away from the scowling wooden face looming in front of him. "I—I'm sorry, Mr. Scarface! Business has been slow, like I said."

Grady swore he saw Scarface's eyes narrow in disgust. That was impossible, of course, because Scarface was nothing more than a puppet made of wood and felt, sitting on the hand of the notorious villain Arnold Wesker, otherwise known as the Ventriloquist.

But, puppet or not, Scarface seemed to have a life of his own. He was the boss of this neighborhood, and today he brought two of his biggest goons—Al and Big Mike—into Grady's shop. Everyone paid Scarface "protection money" to keep their places of business from having a terrible accident, like Big Mike "accidentally" burning down their shops in the middle of the night.

Scarface was a puppet with a mean streak.

"What else ya got?" The wood-and-cloth gangster got so close to Grady's face, he imagined he could smell his bad breath.

"Oh, come now, Scarface," said the jowly, bespectacled little man holding the puppet. "If Mr. Grady says that's all there is, we should take him at his word."

Scarface whipped around so fast, Grady fancied he could hear the pop of knuckles cracking. The puppet was practically spitting sawdust. "You *contradictating* me in front a' da gang, Arnold?"

"Um, I believe the word is *contradicting*. . . ."

"I'm da boss here! Yer just the dummy."

Arnold fell silent. His cheeks darkened to crimson. As Grady watched a man get scolded by his own evil puppet, he wondered, and not for the first time, if maybe it wasn't time to leave Gotham City for good.

"Tell ya what, Grady," Scarface said. "I'll let ya slide just this once. But next time I expect the payment in full, plus interest!"

Scarface pointed at the open cash register. "Okay boys, you all can grab yer share of da loot. Each of you gets a little taste."

Mike and Al both grabbed a handful of cash, careful to give the puppet a wide berth. Meanwhile, Arnold was staring at something high on a dusty shelf in the corner.

"What about you, Arnold? You gonna grab yer share or what?"

"What?" answered Arnold, absently. "Oh, um. Yes, I mean, that is . . ."

The meek little man blinked at Grady past his glasses. "Would it be all right if I, um, helped myself to merchandise? In lieu of cash, I mean."

"What are you talking about, Arnold?" snapped Scarface. "This here pawnshop's filled with nothing but junk!"

Arnold smiled at his puppet. "It's my share, though, Scarface. My decision."

Arnold turned back to the old man. "So, Grady?"

Grady glanced over at the remaining cash and could picture Metropolis Park in his mind. He could taste the street hot dog. If he got to go, he wasn't ever coming back. "Yes! Yes, take whatever you'd like, Mr. Ventriloquist."

"Please, call me Arnold."

Scarface scoffed. "He should call you *chump*, if you ask me."

Nevertheless, Arnold left his share of the cash untouched on the counter and reached up excitedly for the topmost shelf in one dusty corner of Grady's Pawnshop. One could barely see what he was groping for up there in the darkness between the ceiling and the shelf.

What he found was a doll. A porcelain doll, and a very old one at that. The lace frill on her dress had yellowed with age, and a hairline crack extended from her brow to her chin.

"Look, Scarface!" exclaimed Arnold. "She has a scar. Like you!"

"Dat dizzy doll ain't nothing like me," said Scarface. "All those frills and lace look silly."

Although, that wasn't entirely true. There was something about the doll—maybe it was the way her eyes were painted so that they seemed to follow you when you moved—that unnerved Scarface. That is, if puppets had nerves.

The Ventriloquist held the doll up in his free hand. "Scarface, meet Lorelei Lee."

Expertly, the Ventriloquist made the doll do a little curtsy. "Very pleased to meet you, Mister Scarface," said Lorelei, in a soft Southern lilt. The doll's mouth wasn't articulated to move like Scarface's, but the words seemed to come from her. The Ventriloquist really was a master in the craft of throwing his voice.

Lorelei slowly looked around, taking in the shop. "What a lovely day it is for a robbery, don't you all think?"

Scarface saw that Mike and Al were struggling mightily not to laugh.

"Oh, brother," said Mike.

Commissioner Gordon examined a deck of playing cards on the table nearest the cash register. They were faded, with the red-and-white checkered pattern across the front. *An old classic.*

Gordon laughed and said to himself, "Like me."

He flipped the deck over and read the price tag aloud: "'A dollar ninety-nine. Seller not responsible for any missing cards. All sales final.'"

"No wonder this guy is struggling to stay open," said Gordon.

"Grady is struggling because the Ventriloquist is stealing a month's worth of profit every week."

Gordon jumped at the gravelly voice behind him. "Batman. You should try saying hi before you sneak up on a guy. Just once."

Gordon turned to see the Dark Knight standing in the shadows of Grady's Pawnshop. With a flick of his wrist, he produced a black light from a pouch on his belt and began to scan the room.

"My officers already dusted for prints. Besides, we already know who did this."

"I'm not dusting for prints," Batman said.

Gordon gave him a few seconds of silence in which to work. "The owner's name is Grady. We took a statement, but he's still in the back in case you want to talk to him yourself. Minute I heard who the perpetrator was, I knew you'd show up with questions."

"The Ventriloquist and Scarface belong behind bars," said Batman.

Gordon raised an eyebrow. "You talk about that puppet of his like he's alive. Aren't they one and the same?"

"Yes, and no," said Batman. "Arnold Wesker, the Ventriloquist, uses the puppet he calls Scarface to act out the criminal impulses he's ashamed of. Scarface is vicious and devious, whereas Arnold is meek . . . for the most part. But he's gone so far down the rabbit hole that he no longer sees Scarface as a puppet at all. He genuinely sees him as a separate person, albeit one made of wood and cloth. Scarface and the Ventriloquist. Two halves of the same psyche."

Gordon shook his head. "These villains of yours. Makes me miss the good old days of bank robbers in ski masks."

In the rear of the shop, Grady sat in a chair nursing a cup of cold tea. To Gordon's surprise, the man seemed . . . excited? Happy? Certainly not like someone who'd just been robbed by a puppet.

"Mr. Grady," said Batman.

The old man gave a start, then clapped his hands. "Batman! Splendid! Look at my lucky day. First I am robbed, and now I get to meet the famous Batman."

Batman turned to Gordon and gave him a look. Gordon just shrugged. Maybe Grady was in shock.

"Most people wouldn't consider getting robbed to be lucky, Mr. Grady," said Batman.

Grady chuckled. "Oh, but that all depends on what the robbers take."

Gordon cut in. "They took almost a month's earnings in cash."

Grady sighed and his smile faded a bit. "Ah, yes, that part is a pity. But worth it. So very worth it. Worth it to be finally free!"

Batman leaned closer and studied the old man's face. "Mr. Grady, the Ventriloquist stole something from you . . . that you *wanted* stolen, is that what you're saying?"

Grady met the Batman's stare. "Not something. *Someone.*"

"Wait a minute," interrupted Gordon. "You didn't say anything about a kidnapping!"

Grady quickly held up his hands—rattling his teacup and saucer. "No, not a person. Not a flesh-and-blood person, anyway."

Batman straightened and glanced around the shop. His eyes settled on the empty dark space on the highest shelf. An area strangely free of dust. "Mr. Grady, what did the Ventriloquist take?"

The old man's grin returned. He couldn't help it. "He took that horrible doll, Batman. He took *Lorelei Lee!*"

Arnold had never been happier. Of course, Scarface was his best and truest friend, even if he was a bit insensitive sometimes. But for so long it had only been the two of them. Big Mike, Al, and all the other guys who worked for his gang were only there for the money, but Lorelei . . .

Lorelei was like family. Arnold, Scarface, and Lorelei—one big, happy family.

"No, I don't want no milk in my tea!" Scarface was shouting. "Matter of fact, I don't want no *tea*!"

The puppet knocked the plastic teacup off the upturned box that served as a table. "Look at it— it's an empty cup anyway." He turned to glare at Arnold. "Why are we sitting here with this chipped porcelain doll? We should be out there squeezing honest businesses outta their profits."

Lorelei cocked her head. "Scarface, a tea party is *pretend*, dear." The doll paused before adding, "You know, like your *brain*."

The room at the old warehouse hideout went silent. Big Mike and Al stopped their game of dice, leaving the pile of money on an overturned cardboard box that served as a makeshift table. No one so much as breathed. There was only the sound of the crackling fire in the drafty old warehouse's incinerator, which everyone stayed near for warmth.

Scarface whispered to Arnold, "Get me closer to her, ya dummy." Arnold dutifully complied.

"Ahem. Now, what did you say to me, *doll*?"

Lorelei didn't flinch. "Oh, relax, it was just a little teasing. Big bad Scarface can't take a joke?"

Someone snickered. Scarface whipped around to glare at Big Mike. "Something *funny*?"

Big Mike's face went white. "It . . . it wasn't us, boss."

"Whaddaya mean it wasn't youse? If it wasn't you laughing, then who . . ."

Slowly, Scarface turned back around to look up at Arnold, who was busy inspecting the cracks in the ceiling. Anyplace he could look where he didn't have to make eye contact with his other half.

"Hey, dummy."

"Ah, yes, Scarface?"

"Lift me up."

"Okay," said Arnold.

"Closer, like right up to your face . . ."

Scarface whacked Arnold on the nose with his little wooden hand.

"Ow!"

"For laughing at me, ya nitwit."

Arnold's lip quivered. "I didn't mean to! It was just kinda funny."

With Arnold's help, Scarface settled back on the table. "Next time you find something funny—*don't*."

Meanwhile, Lorelei straightened her skirt. "You know, Arnold, maybe Scarface is getting grouchy. Maybe he needs a nap!"

"What?" snapped Scarface.

"Well, uh, Lorelei, I couldn't possibly . . ."

The porcelain doll leaned closer. "Oh yes, you could! It's easy, Arnold. Just set Scarface down and . . . walk away!"

"Walk away?" scoffed Scarface. "Arnold here ain't nothing without me. I'm all he's got, see? I'm all he'll ever have—"

"Do it, Arnold!" Lorelei suddenly snarled in a voice that could have stopped traffic. And what's more, Lorelei shouted at the same time that Scarface was talking.

Big Mike stood up. "Uh, boss. Mr. Ventriloquist, sir. How is it that your puppets are both talking at the same time? Ain't that impossible?"

Arnold looked at Scarface, then he looked at Lorelei. Mike was right. That should not have been impossible.

Scarface looked around, confused. "What are you all talking about? Nobody speaks for me! I speak for the *dummy.*"

"How's it feel to always be called a dummy, Arnold?" asked Lorelei, back to her sweet, soft voice. "Not a very nice word, is it? Maybe it's time you put him in a *time-out.*"

Sweat poured down Arnold's cheeks like water from a faucet. Indecision was painted on his face.

"Now!" snapped Lorelei, and Arnold suddenly jumped to obey. He stepped back from the table. Away from both the doll and the puppet. Scarface toppled over like an empty sack.

Lorelei remained standing.

"Oh—oh, dear!" whined Arnold. "Scarface is going to be so cross with me when he wakes up."

"Poor, dear thing." With a porcelain hand, she tapped the hairline crack that went from her forehead to her chin. "Looks like there's a new Scarface in town."

Lorelei giggled and then turned to look at Big Mike and Al. "Big Mike, be a dear and turn up that incinerator. Al, once it's good and hot, you can do the honors and throw this dummy in with the rest of the trash. *Hee-hee.*"

The two crooks looked at each other, but before they could object, Arnold stepped in.

"L-Lorelei, what are you doing?" he asked.

"What you should have done ages ago, dear," she said sweetly. "I'm ridding you of a problem."

"What? No!" cried Arnold. "You can't burn Scarface! I won't let you!"

Lorelei's painted-on mouth seemed to grin. In the low light, her ink-drawn eyebrows gave her a wicked, haunted look. "Oh, Big Mike? Make sure it's *really* hot!"

"No!" cried Arnold. "Don't listen to her!"

With that, Arnold threw Lorelei across the room. The porcelain doll landed with a clatter behind a stack of crates.

Then he picked up Scarface and cradled him to his chest.

Scarface's wooden hand grabbed Arnold's chin. "Well, ya nitwit, what do ya got to say for yourself?"

"I—I'm sorry, Scarface," said Arnold. "She seemed so nice back in the shop. There was something about her voice. Something musical. Hypnotizing."

"Listen, you and me are a team. Scarface and the Ventriloquist. And I ain't gonna let no creepy doll get in the way of that, got it?"

Arnold nodded obediently.

"Okay," said Scarface. "You guys, go find me that China-cup-in-a-skirt."

"You got it, boss," said Mike. He and Al lumbered over to the other side of the room, and split up to search the floor near the crates. After a minute of searching, Mike came back.

"All's I can find is this," he said, and he held up a piece of porcelain that was no bigger than his thumbnail.

"Lemme see that," said Scarface. Big Mike handed the piece to Arnold. Painted on the porcelain was a delicate, feminine eye.

"Oh, dear. Poor Lorelei," said Arnold. "I should never lose my temper like that."

"Yeah, but where's the rest of her?" asked Scarface.

An eerie, chiming giggle answered him, echoing out of the dark. "Oh, I'm here, Scarface."

Arnold and Scarface looked at each other. "Is that you doing that, Arnold?" asked Scarface.

Arnold shook his head. "No."

Big Mike looked around worriedly. "Hey, Mr. Ventriloquist, could you cut it out? You're kinda scaring me."

"It's not Arnold," said the voice from the darkness. It was cold, and dripping with menace.

The musical quality of her voice was all but gone. "It's me, Lorelei. And I'm not letting you leave."

"All right, enough's enough!" barked Scarface. "Arnold, stop with the whole throwing your voice trick. You're freaking out our boys."

"But it's not me, it's her!" Arnold protested.

Big Mike threw up his hands. "I ain't getting paid enough for this. Bad enough we gotta take orders from a dummy—"

"Hey, watch it!" snapped Scarface.

"That's it, I'm leaving," said Mike. "Al? C'mon."

"Wait!" said Arnold. "Please don't go."

But Al, who was still searching the crates, called out unseen. "Hold on. I think I found . . . how'd that get all the way up there—"

His voice was cut off by the sound of a large crash, like a stack of crates tumbling to the floor.

"Al?" called Mike.

Al didn't answer. Instead, Lorelei crooned from the shadows, "Poor Al is taking a little nap. I'm afraid he's just *buried* in his work."

If Arnold listened closely, he could hear the scuttling of tiny feet running in the dark.

With a groan, Big Mike turned and ran for the stairs. "I'm outta here!"

Scarface looked up at Arnold. "This is all your fault, ya know."

Arnold heaved a sigh. Why was everyone so cross with him?

But just as Mike reached the stairwell, a small shape dashed out of the shadows, tripping him. A rat, maybe? *Or a doll?*

Big Mike tumbled down the steps.

His knees shaking, Arnold peeked over the top of the stairwell. Mike lay at the bottom. The big bruiser moaned like a baby as he cradled an obviously broken leg.

"Now," said Lorelei, from somewhere nearby, "about that fire . . ."

"Oh, Scarface!" whined Arnold. "We should have never made her so angry."

"Will you stop blubbering?" said Scarface. "I gotta think."

"Arnold? Go over and turn that incinerator up," said Lorelei. "Now!"

His eyes brimming with tears, Arnold did as he

was told. She was right; he was weak. He always did what Scarface told him to do because Scarface was stronger than him. Well, now he'd found someone stronger than Scarface.

"Hey!" barked Scarface. "What are you doing, Arnold?"

"I can't help it," sobbed Arnold.

"Ya gotta fight her, pal," said Scarface. "Ya gotta resist!"

But Arnold couldn't. It was like Lorelei had nestled herself deep into his brain. She was calling the shots now. *Arnold* was just a puppet.

Just then, a shattering of broken glass rained down around him. A billowing batlike shape fell from one of the highest windows.

"Batman!" cried Arnold.

The Dark Knight wordlessly took in the scene. Then he asked, "Where's the doll, Arnold?"

Red and blue lights suddenly lit up the remaining windows from outside as multiple police cars came to a speeding halt outside.

"It's Lorelei," sobbed Arnold. "She's evil!"

"Yeah," agreed Scarface. "That's one very, very twisted doll."

"It's just another character you're hiding behind, Arnold," said Batman.

"No! Not this time, Batman," said Arnold. "Honest, she talks on her own. She even walks on her own!"

Batman bent low and scooped up a shape from beneath a pallet of crates. It was a plain porcelain doll. Her face was cracked in several places, and there was now a hole where her left eye used to be.

"Lorelei!" hissed Arnold.

"Good going, Bats," said Scarface. "Toss dat monster into a fire!"

They heard sound of footsteps. Gordon and his men had entered the warehouse.

"Batman!" called Gordon. "Do you have him?"

"Yes. The Ventriloquist isn't going anywhere."

Arnold's shoulders slumped. "Take me in, Batman. I won't fight."

"Hey, speak for yourself!" said Scarface.

"Just put us away behind bars, where"—he eyed the doll warily—"where *she* can't get to us."

"Arnold," said Batman. "It's just a doll. Like Scarface is just a dummy."

"Who you calling a—" but Batman yanked Scarface from Arnold's arms and the dummy's voice went silent. "You're going back to Arkham, Arnold. *Without* Scarface."

"Th-thank you, Batman," said Arnold softly. "I'm ready."

Batman led the Ventriloquist safely down the stairs. Big Mike and Al were loaded onto stretchers. Big Mike had a badly broken leg and Al was in a neck brace, but they were breathing just fine. Gordon put Arnold in handcuffs and by the time he looked back around, Batman was gone. He had disappeared into the night.

"Wish I knew how he did that."

The doll went into an evidence box that was meant to be delivered to Gotham City Police Headquarters, but somehow it never made it that far. The officer responsible for delivering it found himself strangely drawn to the cracked and broken doll. He could almost imagine her sweet, singsong voice talking to him.

It had to be his imagination, right?

Nevertheless, just a few days later, on his daughter's tenth birthday, the officer presented her with a very special gift.

"Her name is Lorelei Lee," he said as she unwrapped the present. "And we are going to be one big, happy family."

Well, that's how poor Arnold ended up back here. Being the more dangerous of the two, I'm sure they have Scarface locked up in maximum security!

As for Lorelei Lee—well, who knows? But I'm sure you can understand why Arnold feels safer in here than he does out there.

And if you come across any one-eyed dolls at the local junk shop, just keep on walking.

But the tour continues!

     Why, just look here at this next cell full of fright and . . . oh. It's **those** two. How disappointing.

     Here in Arkham, you basically have two kinds—your dastardly, themed villains, and . . . their henchmen. The one thing they have in common is that, as bad as it is in here, there's something worse out there!

     Goons and low-rent crooks will join anyone's gang for a buck. Your average henchmen aren't too bright, but these two take the proverbial cake.

     Stately Wayne Manor is synonymous with Gotham City, but the truth is the two couldn't be more different. Set far from the urban sprawl and twisting city streets, Wayne Manor is tucked away miles outside the city in the middle of a vast estate of rolling fields and pleasant woods. With no police for miles around, one would think this luxury home is ripe for the picking by Gotham City's underworld.

     And yet for these many years, Wayne Manor has remained untouched by petty crime. Why? Well, tonight we'll find out in a tale called . . .

TWO

AT HOME WITH THE HENCHMEN!

"For the last time, Dad, I'll be fine here alone. Better than fine."

Damian Wayne, young heir to the leadership of the League of Shadows, sometime Robin, and current middle schooler, stood in the doorway of his father's palatial mansion.

The sun was setting, and his father looked down at his beloved son, as he often did—

with suspicion. "What are you up to, Damian?"

"Nothing!"

His father merely raised an eyebrow.

"Fine, point taken. And under usual circumstances, you'd be right, but tonight I'm attempting to earn your trust. If I mess up, you can ground me until, when? College?"

"Graduation. College *graduation*."

"And why would I risk that?" asked Damian. "Think about it. My logic is sound. I have no ulterior motive."

Here are a few relevant facts about Damian Wayne:

1. For the first twelve years of his life, he was raised by his mother, Talia, as a member of the infamous League of Shadows. He was instructed by the very best minds and trained to fight by the very best masters.

2. Nevertheless, he found the whole thing quite boring once he discovered video games.

3. His father, Bruce Wayne, is secretly Batman. Damian has taken up the role of Robin from time to time, but like many kids his age, he thinks anything his parents do is, by definition, *uncool*, so . . . you see where this is heading.

4. He totally has an ulterior motive.

Bruce scratched his chin. "If Alfred knew I was even thinking about leaving you here alone . . ."

"Alfred is on a well-deserved vacation," said Damian. "And he's overprotective."

"You won't be scared here alone by yourself?"

Damian leveled a look at his father. He was the only middle schooler he knew who didn't mind looking down on adults twice his size.

"Okay, I take it back," said Bruce. "It's just—when I was a kid, growing up in this big empty mansion was sometimes scary."

Damian shrugged. "You just said it's empty. What is there to be scared of?"

Bruce winked conspiratorially. "Well, we have more than a few bizarre items in this old place. In the Batcave, we keep relics from my stranger cases under lock and key, but there are plenty of spooky stories about this old house. In fact, Alfred swears that on certain nights, the ghost of old Thadius Wayne himself walks the halls."

"Thadius Wayne?"

"Your great-great-granduncle. Old Thadius built the garden wing of the house as a gift for his family. But when his youngest son passed away from a fever, Thadius went into mourning and construction was halted. They say Thadius wandered the half-finished garden mumbling for his lost son until he too passed away." Bruce leaned close and whispered, "Some say he was buried there, beneath the garden wing. They just built it over his bones. They say at night his spirit wanders there still. . . ."

Damian blinked, expressionless.

"Nothing?" asked Bruce. "Maybe I didn't tell it as well as Alfred did. Always terrified me when I was your age."

Damian shook his head. "Then you must have been a very gullible child, *Father*."

Bruce sighed. "Fine, you can be home by yourself this evening. But you are to stay *out* of the Batcave and away from the vehicles. I *know* the exact mileage on the Batmobile, the Batwing, the Batboat, the Batcycle, and the Bat-Sub."

Damian's face lit up. "We have a Bat-Sub?"

"Damian!"

The boy waved his hands. "I was just asking, Dad. I don't even like underwater stuff."

(Please note: This is not true. He totally loves underwater stuff.)

Bruce checked his watch. "Selina will kill me if I'm late. The opera is over at ten, so I will be back before eleven. I expect you to be in bed."

"Of course."

"There's a microwave pizza in the freezer. Call me if you get scared."

Bruce put his hand on Damian's head. "Even Batman gets scared sometimes, son."

With that, Bruce got into his car and drove off. Damian waved as his father made the "call me" sign with his fingers. He waited until he could no longer see the red glow of the car's taillights beyond the trees before going back inside. He wanted to be sure his father was truly out of sight.

Damian rubbed his hands together. "Okay then, what's first? Pizza or Bat-Sub? Pizza in the Bat-Sub?"

"For the last time, Lenny, it's gonna be fine!"

Rocko Jones was a two-bit crook, catsitter, and professional henchman-for-hire. He was smarter than your average crook, and good at keeping focus when the heat was on. But as he crouched in the trees half a mile outside Wayne Manor, he was mostly focused on calming his scaredy-cat partner.

"Keep your mind on the job, Lenny. Just think about all that loot sitting unguarded inside that prim and proper mansion. Family jewels, actual *silver* silverware—the sky's the limit, man."

Lenny nodded, but his frown remained unchanged. "Yeah, yeah. Loot."

"So what's the problem?"

Lenny, about a foot taller than Rocko and twice the muscle, glanced over his shoulder at the surrounding woods. "I don't like it outside the city, Rocko. Woods, lonely old houses at night. Didn't you ever see *Demon House*?"

"The movie?"

"Yeah."

"Lenny?"

"Yeah?"

"It's a *movie*."

Lenny just shrugged and looked apprehensively around them.

Rocko needed his partner to focus. Rocko was the brains, and Lenny was the muscle, but muscle isn't any use when it's quivering like jelly.

"Lenny, pal, do you want to go back to doing henchman gigs for weirdos? Getting so bad in Gotham City that a guy like you or me can't make a dishonest living anymore unless you're willing to be some Super-Villain's flunky."

Rocko scooted closer and put his hand on Lenny's meaty shoulder. "You remember the last job we did together? For The Jok—"

Lenny's eyes went wide. "Don't say his name!"

Rocko sighed. "Fine. But you remember what we had to wear? Those nutty big red noses we could hardly breathe through. Plus them big clown shoes that honked when I walked? And I was supposed to be the lookout!"

Lenny chuckled. "Yeah, and all for a truckload of rubber vomit. Seriously, what's he gonna do with sixteen crates of fake puke?"

"I don't know, and I don't *wanna* know. But this is our chance to get out of all that. I've got solid info that billionaire Bruce Wayne is going to the Gotham City Opera Benefit tonight, *and* his butler is out of town. My cousin shines the butler's shoes in Central Station and says he planned this trip to Europe for months. Won't shut up about it."

Suddenly, the trees ahead of them were aglow with a car's headlights. Rocko motioned for them to get down and they crouched just inches off the leafy forest floor. They'd stashed their car a few yards off the side of the road.

The headlights belonged to a sleek black sports car that took the turn with reckless speed. It then slowed, however, and for a moment Rocko feared the car was about to stop right there in the middle of the road.

He held his breath for five seconds, six . . .

And just like that, the tires gave a squeal and the car disappeared off toward Gotham City.

Rocko let out his breath. "Whew. That was Wayne leaving, all right. Only a rich boy drives like that without worrying about cops."

Each man had a small bag slung over one shoulder. "Let's get to work," said Rocko. Inside his bag was a black stocking cap and pants, along with a striped shirt. He put a black mask over his eyes.

He carried a crowbar and a backpack with various lockpicks and tools, plus a couple of extra-extra-large empty satchels for the loot.

"OK, Lenny, you dressed—" He turned around to face his friend, but . . . well, Lenny was dressed, but not as Rocko expected.

Rocko took a deep breath.

"Lenny, what are you wearing?"

His partner looked down at his outfit. "Well, the only DARK clothes I own that are any good for doin' crime are the ones I get from jobs. And I throw away everything except the last one I used. Rocko, you've seen how small my place is—I can't just keep everything. . . ."

Rocko felt his blood pressure rising, but he wouldn't let this ruin things. Nothing would ruin their chance at a really big score. He took a few calming breaths.

"And lemme guess, Lenny. The last job you had. The one whose themed outfit you are now wearing here before me. That job wasn't by any chance for . . . The Penguin?"

Lenny looked down at the ill-fitting tuxedo he'd put on. "Geez, Rocko. How'd you guess?"

For all of Damian's impressive intellect, it took him a surprisingly long time to find the kitchen. Out of habit, he first simply sat at the dining room table and waited for the pizza to be brought to him. After a few minutes, he realized that with no Alfred around and no Bruce, no one would *bring* him *anything*.

But the microwave was easy to operate, and it was not long before the cheese began to bubble and the kitchen was filled with pizza aroma. He'd barely sat down with his first piping-hot slice of gooey goodness and a stack of comics when a blinking red light caught his attention.

The security system.

The monitor was at Bruce's height, so Damian had to scoot over a chair and hop up to see what the alert was about. There appeared to be a man in a tuxedo stuck on the fence outside.

Damian scratched his chin like his father and looked again. The tuxedo man was still there, but now he wasn't alone. Another man dressed in black was behind him, trying to help him get unstuck.

Was this Father's idea of a practical joke? Doubtful, because Father had zero sense of humor. He even messed up dad jokes, and dad jokes were exhaustingly simple.

When Damian looked closer, he could see the tuxedo man's face, although it was contorted in pain as he wiggled around on the fence.

So, it was a man in black and a man dressed somewhat like a chorus-line singer from an old movie. Had Batman's enemy The Penguin discovered Father's secret identity and sent assassins? Now *that* was exciting!

The man in the tuxedo freed himself from the fence and landed inside the courtyard with a painful thump.

A message appeared on the security screen: INTRUDERS HAVE BREACHED THE PERIMETER. LAUNCH-ING COUNTERMEASURES COUNTDOWN.

Too bad, thought Damian. *Father's security was state of the art, and would undoubtedly have the two assassins trapped in no time. Sleeping gas, a cage. The evening's entertainment over and the intruders caught. Unless . . .*

Damian reached up and pushed the red Cancel button on the screen.

A new message appeared. PASSWORD, PLEASE?

Damian grinned. Father's passwords were exceedingly simple. He typed *A . . . C . . . E.*

Ace the Bat-Hound. Father's old dog.

The countdown stopped. COUNTERMEASURES CANCELED, the message read. SECURITY SYSTEMS GOING OFFLINE.

The monitor went back to its standard warm, dull glow.

Excellent. Damian hopped down from his chair and rubbed his hands together in anticipation. He would defend Father's home, and he would do so on a level playing field. But he couldn't be seen as Robin. If he faced them in open combat as Robin, it would provoke suspicion. People would wonder what the Boy Wonder was doing at Wayne Manor.

Damian would have to get creative, but first things first.

Stopping assassins is so much more fun than a slice of pizza—but that didn't stop him from taking a before running off to meet the intruders.

The plan was to get over the fence, make a run for it in case of dogs, and not stop until they'd reached the house. But after the fiasco back at the fence, Rocko and Lenny were winded before they'd made it halfway across the grounds. Thankfully, there wasn't an attack dog in sight.

Lenny sat in the grass catching his breath while Rocko braced his hands on his knees.

"Lenny, why don't you take that stupid outfit off? Ain't you hot?"

"Burning up. But this here so-called penguin suit's bulletproof, fireproof, and has extra padding. Why, I bet I could take a punch from the Batman and not even feel it!"

"Batman's the last thing we got to worry about

this far from Gotham City. But if you get caught on another fence, I'm leaving you behind."

"Don't say that, Rocko. It's not nice."

Rocko wanted to ask what business a couple of crooks-for-hire like them had being *nice*, but instead he just offered Lenny a hand up off the grass. "Only thing sillier than a crook in a tuxedo is a crook sitting on his rear in a tuxedo. C'mon."

Huddled outside the ground-floor window, Lenny put his face up against the glass. "Looks dark in there."

"'Cause it's empty, said Rocko. "Stand back."

He took his crowbar up with both hands. "This is a very sophisticated breaking-and-entering device!" He swung the iron crowbar at the window, and . . .

. . . dropped it with a yelp as the impact vibrated up and down his arms.

The glass wasn't even scratched.

"What kinda glass is that?" moaned Rocko.

Lenny tapped on it. "Pretty solid. Maybe we should come back another time with better tools."

At that precise moment, the front door swung open wide.

"Get down!" whispered Rocko, and the two of them hid as best they could in the house's shadow.

"No one's coming out, Rocko."

It was true. The front door to Wayne Manor was now wide open. But no one was in sight.

Rocko peeked around the corner. "Musta been the wind. These old houses, ya know."

Lenny wasn't convinced. "An old drafty house with unbreakable windows? I dunno, Rocko."

But Rocko was already stepping though the threshold. Far from a dusty, drafty old mansion, Wayne Manor was spotless. Shining brass lamp fixtures lined a grand central staircase. The brightly polished wood floors didn't so much as squeak beneath Rocko's feet. And he had to admit, it would take more than a draft to blow open the heavy, reinforced front door.

It was dark, however, and the lamps were all out. Not a single sign of human activity.

"Rocko," whined Lenny. "I wanna go back to Gotham City."

"No one's home. There's nothing to worry about."

Lenny followed the staircase with his eyes until the steps disappeared into the darkness above.

"I'm not worried about people. Not living ones, anyway."

The words had barely left Lenny's mouth when he heard a noise coming from the steps.

Thump. Thump.

"Rocko! You hear that?"

Thump. Thump. Thump.

Coming closer. Something was coming down the steps.

Rocko appeared at Lenny's side. "What the heck is that?"

It came into sight now. A child's ball, no bigger than Lenny's fist, was bouncing toward them slowly, down the steps.

Thump. Thump.

It rolled to a stop by their feet.

Rocko stooped to pick it up.

Scrawled across the ball in blood was a message: GET OUT.

"Let's go, Rocko!"

"Waitaminute." Rocko rubbed at the words with his thumb. "It's not blood. It's paint."

"Who cares?" cried Lenny.

A child's wailing voice cried out from the dark, "Get out!"

Tumble! Tumble! Tumble!

Rocko and Lenny looked up in time to see the red metal wagon crashing down heavily on top of them. They tried to move out of the way, but Lenny turned and slammed right into Rocko.

The two burglars fell down in a tangle when the wagon smashed into them. Rocko was pinned beneath Lenny, grunting as he struggled to get out from under his accomplice.

Meanwhile, hidden in the darkness at the top of the stairs, Damian winced at the sound of breaking glass. He hoped he hadn't just smashed Alfred's prized collection of glass unicorns, because it certainly *sounded* like he'd just smashed Alfred's prized collection of glass unicorns.

When Damian had discovered the old attic a few weeks back, he'd been disappointed to find it contained mostly childish toys. Probably Bruce's from when he was a boy. Nothing sentimental about that. From what Damian could tell from the few so-called "horror movies" he'd seen, adults paid flesh-and-blood children little mind. But *ghost* children were, for some reason, terrifying.

He expected the thieves to last another two minutes, maybe less. The one in the tuxedo panicked and ran for the nearest hallway that headed toward the dining room.

If this had been Mother's house—the Grand Fortress of the League of Shadows— Damian would have had plenty to play with, such as spiked caltrops, and even flaming oil. But Father's house was so boring, except for the Batcave, and that was off-limits.

Damian slid down the banister with glee. This would still be fun. He would hassle and harangue the two, unseen, until he'd chased them right out of the house. A few more ghostly wails and perhaps a smashed plate or two should do the trick. Hopefully they wouldn't run *too* fast.

Damian wanted to have some more fun.

The two thieves came flying through the kitchen door—Lenny in mad panic and Rocko right on his heels. But suddenly, Lenny skidded to an abrupt halt . . . Rocko nearly barreled into him.

"What's the matter with you?" Rocko panted. "First you go off screaming, and now . . ."

His voice trailed off as he looked down at the scene. They'd run blindly into the mansion's large kitchen. A small table sat against on wall.

Three quarters of a pizza was uneaten. Rocko picked it up. "Your ghost doesn't like the crusts. And it's still warm."

Lenny's face turned red. "So . . ."

"So, this ghost is human. Someone's just trying to scare us away."

Lenny's face went from red to purple with rage. Lenny was finally angry, and no one wanted to mess with Lenny when he was angry. "Whoever it is will be wishing they were a ghost!"

They crept out of the kitchen and into the long hallway they'd come from. "Here," whispered Rocko, pointing to a pair of tall potted plants. "We'll hide there, and when whoever it is comes through, we nab them!"

Lenny nodded and cracked his knuckles. "No one makes a fool of me."

Rocko looked at Lenny in his ridiculous suit but said nothing.

Damian looked at his reflection in the foyer mirror and sighed. With a little more time, he could've added some fake blood, perhaps an oozing wound or two. As it was, he'd have to make the most of his pallid reflection—provided by a generous helping of baking flour taken from the storage pantry. The deathly pale ghost boy of Wayne Manor!

Damian sneezed and stirred up a vast cloud of powdery flour.

Outside the kitchen, Damian found the child's ball with the "bloody" message in paint he had left for them earlier. The crooks must've dropped it there, so they couldn't have gone far. But as he approached the garden wing, the house lamps flickered and suddenly went out.

Damian thought it was strange, because there were no storms nearby that he knew of. Were the crooks more capable than he'd given them credit for? That just made the evening all the more fun.

Damian held up the ball and gave the League of Assassins salute. "Worthy opponents, I honor you!" he said, then hurried off after them, leaving white footprints in his wake.

While Lenny and Rocko hid behind the plants in the hallway, Lenny started to get nervous. The lights had gone out. But Rocko reminded him about the pizza, and he found his courage again.

It didn't take long for them to hear the sounds of approaching footsteps. They were soft, almost quiet. Someone sneaking, perhaps.

Lenny whispered, "I'm cold."

Rocko hushed him with a look. He was right, though. It was weirdly chilly in this hallway compared to rest of the house.

The footsteps got louder. Their pretend ghost was only a few feet away now. Rocko held up his fingers. *One. Two* . . .

The tall windows overlooking the garden let in enough moonlight to see by, and Damian had no trouble spotting the two figures hiding behind the potted plants in the long hallway. He knew he was in no real physical danger from these two clowns. He'd been trained by Batman himself and had grown up in the League of Shadows. But he was hoping that the sight of this ghastly white "ghost child" would send them running without the need

for a physical confrontation that would risk expos-
ing him as a living boy.

Cautiously, he crept forward until he was a
mere few feet away from them. But then, quite
surprisingly, the two crooks leapt out from behind
the plants. They hadn't been hiding from him—
they'd been waiting to ambush him! And here he
was armed with nothing but a child's rubber ball.

If Damian's mother found out, he would never
live it down. Heir to the League of Shadows
ambushed by a pair of second-rate burglars?

Nothing to do but follow through with the

plan. He held out his arms like they did in zombie movies and began to moan. *"Get ouuuut!"*

To his delight and surprise, the crooks froze in place. Looks of absolute terror spread across their faces as they stared at him. A crowbar fell from one of their hands, clattering onto the floor.

Damian worked up another ghostly groan, but the two men already turned and fled. This time they ran for the garden door, and after a few seconds of fumbling with the lock, they burst through the door and took off into the night. They ran with no intention of coming back.

"Well," said Damian. "That takes care of those two. . . ."

The words died on his lips, however. The hairs on the back of his neck suddenly stood up as a chilly breeze blew toward him. The breeze wasn't coming from the now-open garden door. It was coming from *behind* him, like a cold breath against his head.

In a flash he remembered the two crooks from just moments before, as they'd stared at him in horror. No, not at him. Their eyes had been affixed in his general direction, but they'd been staring at something . . . above him.

Slowly, Damian looked up.

And there it was, a figure hovering over his shoulder. At first glance, it looked like a man, tall and gaunt. But when Damian looked closer, he noticed the strange clothing, like something out of another century. And that the clothing was not just old in style, but it was *old*. Moldering, rotted in places, and inside those gaping holes, the flesh beneath was pale and mottled.

The figure was reaching out for Damian.

Despite his years of training, and the iron will inherited from both parents, Damian's legs buckled beneath him and he fell to his knees, his lip quivering in fear.

Long, bony fingers reached out and . . . snatched the ball out of Damian's hands. "This. Doesn't. Belong. To. You."

And just like that, the phantom vanished, taking the ball with him.

Bruce returned to the mansion early that night. He had to admit, he was secretly pleased when he got Damian's text to come home. As Batman, he knew Gotham City needed him, but it was also nice to be needed as a father now and again. When he opened the front door, Damian threw himself into Bruce's arms.

"Father," Damian said. "Are those your old toys up in the attic?"

"The attic? No, I think those have been there

since before I was born. I think they might even date back to old Thadius's day. I never liked going up there myself. It was spooky. Why do you ask?"

Damian went into the study without answering and returned with the red wagon. "I'm putting this back, okay?" he shouted, but Bruce didn't think he was talking to him. "Do you hear me? I won't touch it again. Any of it!" Then he started dragging the wagon up the stairs.

Just when I think I understand that boy . . . , thought Bruce. He grinned and shook his head. *At least he didn't break anything while I was gone.*

"Oh, and Father," called Damian over his shoulder. "Tell Alfred I owe him some unicorns."

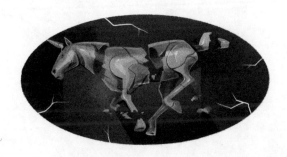

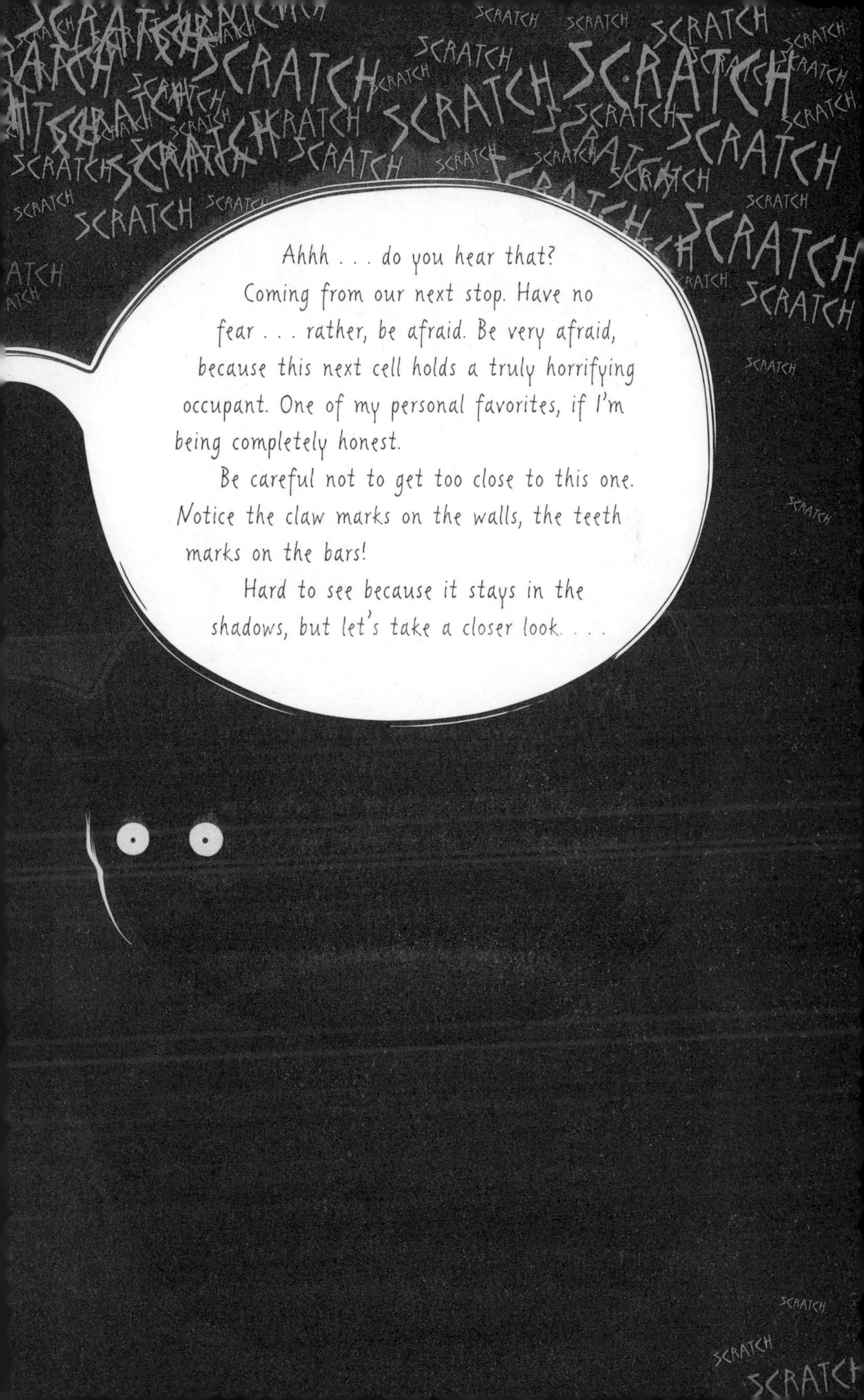
SCRATCH SCRATCH SCRATCH SCRATCH
Ahhh . . . do you hear that? Coming from our next stop. Have no fear . . . rather, be afraid. Be very afraid, because this next cell holds a truly horrifying occupant. One of my personal favorites, if I'm being completely honest.
Be careful not to get too close to this one. Notice the claw marks on the walls, the teeth marks on the bars!
Hard to see because it stays in the shadows, but let's take a closer look . . .
SCRATCH SCRATCH SCRATCH

THREE

WHAT LURKS WITHIN

Gotham Academy is nearly as old as Gotham City itself. A prestigious boarding school for the young heirs of the city's rich and powerful, over the years the academy has become known as a home for more than the children of the elite.

The good *and* the bad.

And while any place as old as Gotham Academy is bound to have its share of rumors and legends, this school's were dark indeed. The stories were full of secret societies and mysterious disappearances. Stories of chance encounters with ghosts and specters from the past.

However, it was not by chance that Barbara Gordon, aka Batgirl, found herself sitting in Gotham Academy's fifth-period advanced biology class. She was there with a secret purpose.

And so far, everything was going to plan.

Zzzspit!

"O.M.G., bull's-eye! Spitball directly on the cheek! Well, almost to plan."

Barbara took a deep, steadying breath and wiped the soggy lump of paper off her face. Jackson Cobblepot, the rich nephew of the notorious Oswald Cobblepot, laughed as Barbara turned to face him. He was flanked by Nell Binder, who had the decency to hide behind her long black bangs, and Felix Maroni, a skinny kid who wore a constant smirk. Jackson wasn't even trying to conceal the straw he'd pilfered from fourth-period lunch. Unlike his short, round uncle, Jackson was big for his age and muscular. He liked to brag about being a trophy-winning black belt in karate.

Barbara had five of them.

But she simply sank down farther into her seat and fumed. Batman's orders were to keep a low profile. He wanted her to stay focused on her mission, and her mission was not Jackson Cobblepot. It was the gaunt, glasses-wearing professor who was just now making his way into the classroom. He was five minutes late, Barbara noted.

Dr. Kirk Langstrom cleared his throat and gently asked the other students to please take their seats. Jackson made a show of being the last to sit.

"Good afternoon, class," said Dr. Langstrom. "Today we are going to continue our discussion of the concept of spontaneous adaptation. This *will* be on the test, so you might want to take notes."

As the other students groaned, Barbara took out her own biology notebook. On the outside were the standard doodles of peace signs, hearts, the names of her favorite bands, and a few bats. But inside, where she should be taking biology notes, were notes of a different kind— observations of Kirk Langstrom. His daily habits, whether he looked tired in class—unkempt or unshaven. Anything that might point to unusual stress in his life.

She wrote the date and "five minutes late."

Barbara would ace the test, of course. Batman required everyone he worked with to be studying graduate-level biology, along with a host of other topics. It didn't matter if you were seventeen-year-old Batgirl or middle schooler Robin. (Damian probably already had his doctorate degree.)

As the lesson went on, Barbara studied Dr. Langstrom. He did seem tired, but not overly so. Nothing that a bad night's sleep wouldn't explain. He seemed to lose his train of thought a few times, and he had to rub his eyes beneath his glasses to get it back again.

Hmm. Memory a little foggy, doc?

Barbara wrote it down.

Lost as she was in watching his every move, she found herself startled by how quickly the time flew by. Barbara was brought back to Earth by the rustle of books being quickly slipped into backpacks and the scooting of chairs.

"Ah, one more thing, class," said Dr. Langstrom. "I've been asked by Principal Sears to once again warn you that Hillman Belltower is off-limits to students. It's pledge week, and I know that some clubs like to make a challenge of climbing the so-called 'Hangman's' Belltower, but it's condemned for a *reason*. The belltower is *not* haunted—that's unscientific nonsense—but it *is* old and in disrepair."

Students started filing out of the classroom when, uncharacteristically, Dr. Langstrom raised his voice.

"Someone is going to get hurt!" he said.

There was an awkward silence as the class exchanged glances. Some nodded. A few mumbled in agreement. Luckily, the bell rang and Dr. Langstrom hurried out of class.

As they packed up, Jackson whispered to his friends, barely loud enough for Barbara to hear, "We'll see who gets hurt, you freak."

What did he mean by that? Did Jackson

Cobblepot somehow, improbable as it seemed, know Dr. Langstrom's secret?

Barbara wanted to see where Dr. Langstrom had hurried off to, but Nell caught Barbara's eye.

"Jackson didn't mean anything by it," Nell said.

"Spitball to the face is all just fun and games, huh?" answered Barbara, and Nell's cheeks darkened. "Look, Nell, why do you even hang out with those jerks? You're not at all like Jackson and Felix."

Nell looked cautiously over her shoulder, but the two of them were alone for the time being. The rest of the students had already headed to next period. "Jackson, Felix, and I have more in common than you think."

"Like what?"

"It's complicated, but our families are all . . . business friends, I guess."

Barbara already knew about the Cobblepots and the Maronis. The Cobblepot family had produced The Penguin, and the Maronis were Gotham City's most infamous crime family, but Barbara had never heard the name Binder before. So Barbara decided to ask.

"Are your parents well-off?"

"No," said Nell. "My dad runs a lock shop. It's the family business. Felix's parents are kind of . . . investors in it."

Barbara knew what that meant. The Maronis owned a piece of several businesses all over Gotham City. But it was a racket, and one that was never good for shop owners.

"Anyway, Jackson and Felix are helping me get a job that'll cover school tuition so my dad doesn't have to worry about it."

"A job?" asked Barbara. "You mean like work-study?"

"Something like that," answered Nell. The girl wouldn't make eye contact with Barbara now. But while Barbara had the sense that the girl wasn't telling her the whole truth, Nell didn't seem to be lying, exactly. She was leaving out something important.

"Anyway, I don't want to be late for class," said Nell. "I just wanted to say sorry about Jackson."

With that, Nell turned and hurried out of the room. Barbara almost called after her, told her to wait. Nell wasn't a bad girl; in fact, she was someone Barbara could see as a friend.

But she wasn't here to make friends. She was on a mission that didn't have anything to do with Nell Binder. Making friends now would just complicate things. It might even put innocent people in danger.

So Barbara gathered her things and headed off to her own next period. But the bell rang just as she reached the door, and smug Professor Lyons was waiting for her with a tardy slip.

High school really was the worst.

"You owe me, Batman," she muttered under her breath. "You owe me big-time."

Up in her room, Barbara entered the combination on her "suitcase" and took out the tablet Batman had entrusted her with. She placed her index finger on the fingerprint scanner.

The screen lit up with a bat-symbol. Barbara rolled her eyes. Batman was all about branding.

"Fingerprint confirmed. Body temperature confirmed."

Barbara had once asked why the tablet took her temperature, and Damian theorized that it was to prevent someone from using her finger, and *only* her finger, to gain access.

Damian was a weird kid . . . even if he did make sense sometimes.

After a moment of static, a brooding cowled face took up the screen.

"You're late with your report," said Batman. He was coming to her from the cockpit of the Batmobile, both hands tightly gripping the wheel.

"Well, I saw on the news that you were chasing Mr. Freeze all over downtown, so I thought I'd give it a few."

"Irrelevant. I can multitask. How's your surveillance of Kirk Langstrom going?"

"He sometimes comes in late. Looks pretty much exhausted."

"Being a tired teacher is no crime. Langstrom deserves this chance."

"He turned himself into a bat!"

"A Man-Bat," said Batman. "And it was an accident of science. When he's himself, Kirk Langstrom is a valuable member of society. He's fought the beast inside him, and it seems he's finally won. Now he needs people to trust him. I trust him."

Barbara arched an eyebrow. "If you trust him so much, why have me spy on him?"

"I trust Langstrom. I don't trust Man-Bat."

Barbara looked down at her notes. "You're right, being tired isn't any kind of proof. I'll suit up and patrol the school tonight. If Langstrom's taking any late-night flights, I'll know it."

"Good plan. But be careful. If he is transforming again, Man-Bat is dangerous. Very dangerous."

After weeks of spitballs, crowded hallways, and, *ugh*, gym class, it felt good to be in the suit again. Batman thought the yellow boots were a silly fashion statement, but what was she supposed to wear—high heels?

Besides, the shoes said she wasn't just a girl version of the Dark Knight. She was her own crime fighter, her own Super Hero. Barbara had earned the right to the name Batgirl.

And if the sneakers were a fashion statement, then they were a statement against the gloom and decay of Gotham Academy. Perched atop the gabled roof of the academy's Wayne Hall, Batgirl studied the campus from up high. The academy looked like a place out of time—with its twisting tower ramparts and gabled roofs. Batgirl had to be extra careful not to lose her footing on a loose shingle. The roof creaked so ominously in places, she worried it might give way beneath her. The only place with a better vantage point was Hillman Belltower, or Hangman's Tower, as the kids called it. Legend was that the tower was built atop the site of an old hangman's gallows back when Gotham City was little more than a frontier town. People claimed they could see ghostly bodies hanging from the belltower at night.

Plans to renovate the historic tower always seemed to fall apart, so the tower just sat there, locked and boarded up. Buildings were that way all over campus, as if the old school refused to *let* itself be changed for the better. Besides the students and teachers, the only things that Barbara had seen were the rats and the climbing ivy that choked the outer walls.

Batgirl swept her gaze back over the campus, past the quad. The late September nights were getting longer and starting to hint that fall had arrived. There was a chill in the air once the sun went down. It was back-to-school weather; it was Halloween-is-right-around-the-corner weather.

Batgirl groaned at the thought of still being on this mission at Halloween. One more month of eleventh grade and she wouldn't need a costume—she would be a zombie for real.

The clock was creeping up on midnight and windows all the across campus were dark. Except for the science building. There was a single light on in an open window on the third floor. The shade was drawn and it fluttered in the night breeze.

"Dr. Langstrom, I presume?" Batgirl said to herself. "Awfully late to be up grading papers."

Batgirl did a quick inventory of her micro Utility Belt. Hand-to-hand combat with Man-Bat was not on her bucket list, and she hoped it wouldn't come to that. Maybe Kirk Langstrom was just suffering from good old insomnia. Maybe he'd gone from Man-Bat to night owl.

As the thought flitted across Batgirl's mind, she heard a noise coming from Dr. Langstrom's window. It sounded like a struggle, followed by breaking of glass.

Game time.

Batgirl looped a Batrope around the sturdiest gable she could find and rappeled down the wall

to the ground beneath. She kept one eye on Dr. Langstrom's open window as she hurried across the cobblestone courtyard that made up the quad.

But no sooner had she reached the science building than the door burst open. Batgirl threw herself flat against the wall as three figures came bolting out. They were dressed in dark clothing, and when one of them lagged behind and threw a glance over their shoulder, Batgirl saw a white, grinning skull instead of a face.

"Nell!" called one of the others in a harsh whisper. "Come on!"

Nell? Batgirl recognized the voice. It made her stomach sink.

Stupid, stupid, stupid!

The three skull-faced figures ran for Hangman's Belltower. Batgirl started to give chase when she heard a pained moan come from inside. Someone was hurt. The skulls would have to wait.

Batgirl sprinted into the building and up the stairs to the lab, taking them two at a time. She found the door ajar and Dr. Langstrom lying on the floor. Batgirl ran to his side. He was alive but dazed. Someone had given him a nasty bump on the forehead. Batgirl rolled up his jacket and gently tucked in under his head. Dr. Langstrom looked up at Batgirl with unfocused eyes.

Batgirl did a quick scan of the lab. Someone had knocked over a rack of test tubes, and a small safe beneath Dr. Langstrom's desk was wide open.

Had Nell and her friends broken into Dr. Langstrom's lab? But why?

Batgirl remembered something Nell had said, that Jackson and Felix were helping Nell get a job. Batgirl should have seen it earlier. What sort of job would The Penguin's nephew and the heir to the Maroni crime family offer someone like Nell?

Maybe breaking and entering? Theft?

Dr. Langstrom moaned again, and this time he mumbled a few words. "My . . . my serum . . ."

His serum? Oh no.

"Doctor, you stay here," said Batgirl. "I have to stop some kids from doing something stupid."

Batgirl didn't bother with the stairs. She leapt

from the open window and used her reinforced cape to glide safely to the ground. It was one of the neater tricks Batman had taught her.

Nell and her friends had been heading toward Hangman's Tower, so that was where Batgirl went. The door to the tower was boarded up and decorated with fresh graffiti depicting a stick figure dangling from a rope, like something a child would draw in the game hangman. But the boards on one side of the door had been pried loose so that there was enough space for a grown man to squeeze through. There was more than enough room for a Batgirl.

Inside, it was dark and musty. There was even more graffiti on the walls, and the floor was littered with cans and empty chip bags, plus a few old pizza boxes. Someone had stuck candles here and there. Some were melted down to nubs.

So, this is where the cool kids come to party, huh? No wonder I've never been in here, she thought.

A winding stairway disappeared amongst cobwebbed rafters, curling its way up the length of the tower. The stairs were stained with some suspicious-looking mold, but they appeared sturdy enough. Batgirl began the long climb up, wincing at every creak and groan the wood gave beneath her feet.

It wasn't long before she heard voices. Someone up there was getting into an argument.

"You didn't have to hit him, Jackson."

"What? Did you want to explain to Langstrom what we were doing in his lab, and why Nell here was cracking his safe? Not my fault he wandered in before we were finished."

Breaking into his safe? Of course. Nell said her dad owned a lock shop. He must've worked as a safecracker, too. And Nell had learned the "family business" from him.

Barbara found the three of them in the belfry at the very top of the tower. Though they were still wearing those creepy skull masks, Batgirl knew who they were—Jackson Cobblepot, Felix Maroni, and, sadly, Nell Binder.

Nell was looking askance at a vial in her hands. Inside was a sickly-looking green liquid that emitted a dull glow. "I cracked Langstrom's safe because The Penguin, er, your *uncle*, said there'd be money. Enough to get my dad out of debt."

Jackson shrugged. "There will be. Just as soon as my uncle sells that stuff to the highest bidder. In the meantime, we stash it up here until my uncle can collect."

So that was the plan. The Penguin wanted Dr. Langstrom's serum so he could sell it to some idiot who probably wanted to make an army of Man-Bats. And he was using a bunch of kids to do his dirty work for him. Time to put a stop to this.

"All right, that's enough," she said, stepping out of the shadows and bringing herself to her full height. Though shorter than Batman, Batgirl was all lean muscle, and she carried herself like someone who knew how to fight—because she did. Plus, the bat-symbol on her chest did wonders. Everyone in Gotham City knew what that symbol meant. Everyone knew who *she* was.

"Bat-Lady!" breathed Felix.

"Bat*girl*," said Batgirl, through gritted teeth.

Felix threw up his hands. "I give up! I give up!"

Now, that was more like it. Batgirl wore her best Batman scowl and put her hands on her hips. "Hand over the serum."

For just a moment, it looked like Jackson would do the smart thing and surrender, but then Batgirl heard a voice behind her.

"Give that back! You don't know what you're doing!"

Dr. Langstrom came up the stairs. Batgirl had been so focused on the kids that she hadn't heard him approach. Dr. Langstrom's face was pale and feverish. Probably had a concussion from the blow he'd taken.

Batgirl hoped it was just a concussion. He did not look good.

"Doctor Langstrom, you shouldn't be up here," said Batgirl.

But he barely registered her presence. He was laser-focused on the serum in Nell's hand.

"That's not what you think!" he said. "It's different now. I had to use it to make this, but it altered the formula. . . ."

Batgirl saw now that Dr. Langstrom was holding a metal syringe. A weapon? The situation was about to get out of control.

"Nell," said Batgirl. "Do what he says and give the serum back. It's not too late."

Nell looked down at the vial in her hands. "I—I'm sorry. My dad owes the Maronis so much money that they'll never let him go straight."

She held out the vial.

"But he'd be ashamed to see me like—" Nell paused. "Wait, how did you know my name?"

Jackson then moved faster than Batgirl would've thought possible for a guy his size. He grabbed at the vial.

"No!" he shouted. "We're not giving it back!"

But Nell was stronger than she looked, and for a moment the two of them struggled over the serum. Jackson wrenched it out of Nell's hands, and they fell into Felix, knocking him backward.

Off the belfry. Off the top of the tower.

The boy barely had time to scream as Batgirl leapt after him. For an instant, they were both in a free fall high above the courtyard. But Batgirl wrapped an arm around Felix and used her other hand to fire her Bat-Grapnel up at the giant bell. Luckily, the bell held. And luckily, Felix was scrawny for his age.

"Hold on!" she grunted as the mechanized grappling hook hoisted them back up to the belfry.

Felix whimpered as he climbed to safety. Batgirl lifted herself up behind him.

Dr. Langstrom was on the floor, sobbing. Nell had backed herself into a corner near the stairs, and Jackson . . . he was on his hands and knees. The vial lay shattered around him, and faint wisps of green smoke were carried away in the breeze.

"What happened?" said Batgirl, but she had a sinking feeling she already knew the answer.

"The formula altered," Dr. Langstrom was saying between sobs. "Turned into a gas . . ."

The Man-Bat serum was a gas? And Jackson had just gotten a face full of it.

Some kind of seizure shook Jackson, and he screamed. His skin rippled as the muscles beneath swelled. The fabric of his clothes tore at the seams. His ears grew long, and Jackson's cries of pain became snarls of rage as his face contorted into a fanged muzzle.

As Batgirl watched in horror, Jackson's arms popped and stretched into long leathery wings, like he was being pulled apart on some medieval torture instrument. But it was no device doing this to him—

it was Dr. Langstrom's serum, and it was remaking Jackson into something else.

A Man-Bat.

The worst was Jackson's eyes—the look of terror and pain in his eyes right up until the moment they turned bloodred.

The Man-Bat screeched and bared its fangs.

"Everyone out!" called Batgirl.

The Man-Bat reached for the fleeing kids with a hungry look on its face.

Felix froze in fear. He stood there staring at the beast that had once been his friend.

Batgirl threw herself between Felix and the Man-Bat. Seeing a new target, the creature lunged, and she barely managed to dodge its raking claws.

She had a split second to act. With her yellow boots a blur, she aimed a roundhouse kick . . .

. . . directly into the center of Felix's rear end, shoving him forward and out of the Man-Bat's reach. The boy screamed and followed Nell down the steps.

Good. Civilians out of the way. Now to just—

Before she could even complete the thought, a pair of claws yanked her off her feet and threw her. The only reason she didn't tumble out of the belfry was that she hit the giant bell.

The wind had gotten knocked out of her and

she fell, barely managing to grab the rope to keep herself from falling down the winding staircase.

The massive brass bell rang with a loud *GONG!*

The sound set Batgirl's ears ringing, but it did far worse to Man-Bat's super-sensitive ears. The creature howled in pain, then leapt off the tower—and flew off into the night.

Batgirl climbed the rope and lay on the floor of the belfry, gasping for breath.

"All according to plan," she said, and winced at how much her ribs hurt to even talk.

"Batgirl?"

Kirk Langstrom helped her up. "Are you hurt?"

"Only my pride, doctor," said Batgirl. "And my shoulder. Plus I might have a cracked rib or two. But why on earth were you keeping your Man-Bat serum in a school lab?"

Dr. Langstrom stared off into the night. "This is my fault. I needed access to a laboratory to work on a cure. And to fashion a cure, you need to study the disease."

He looked down at the metal syringe in his hands. "I have the Man-Bat—*my* Man-Bat—under control, but it's always there, waiting to break free.

95

And if it works, what's in this syringe will rid me of the monster for good."

The antidote.

"Well, we have a whole new monster to deal with now," said Batgirl, and at that moment they heard a shriek and a heavy thump as something large landed on the roof above them.

"He's come back to finish the job," whispered Dr. Langstrom. "Man-Bats hold a grudge."

Batgirl took out a handful of sleeping gas pellets from her belt. "That cure of yours—do you have enough for two doses?"

Langstrom paled. "No. With the time and

resources, I can make more. It's got about a fifty-percent chance of working at all."

"A coin toss?"

"A coin toss that could give me my life back."

Batgirl nodded. After a moment's hesitation, Langstrom handed her the syringe. "For Jackson. I'm still a teacher, you know. The well-being of my students comes first."

Batgirl tucked the syringe into her belt. "Stay back. I'm going to lure him close."

But there was no need, because the roof of the belfry was suddenly ripped off in chunks as the Jackson Man-Bat tore it apart to get to his prey.

Dr. Langstrom stared up at the beast with a mixture of revulsion and pity. No fear. He was finally facing a version of the monster he had been fighting for years. Finally seeing it for himself.

None of that would stop him from getting eaten, however, so Batgirl called, "Hey, bat-boy!"

With a flip, she wrapped both arms around its neck. "Gotcha!"

The Man-Bat snarled and leapt from the belfry again—this time with Batgirl.

The beast tried to shake Batgirl off, flapping

its wings in fury. It was all she could do to hold on with both hands. She dared not reach for the syringe at her belt.

Luckily, the Man-Bat decided it would be easier to eat her if it wasn't so busy flapping its wings, so it landed atop the tall Wayne Library, on the very edge of the roof, not far from Batgirl's original lookout perch.

Now that it had landed, it didn't need its arms for flying, so it could reach around and pluck the annoying Batgirl off its back.

But that also meant Batgirl didn't need her hands to hold on.

Long claws scraped along her sides as the beast grabbed her, pinning her arms to her sides. The Man-Bat lifted her up, glaring at its prey with those red eyes, its mouth opening wide. . . .

"I call . . . *heads* . . ." Batgirl wheezed as she struggled to breathe in the creature's grasp. The Man-Bat paused, then noticed the empty syringe in its arm. The *empty* syringe.

The change began immediately. Fur turned to skin. Bones and muscle contracted, and the red eyes turned hazel once again. For a moment,

Jackson stood there on the edge of the roof, watching his body become recognizable as *human* again. She felt sorry for the boy, despite it all. The look of horror in his eyes was hard to watch.

It was all too much for him. Jackson's eyes rolled back into his head and he fainted. His limp body rolled right off the roof's edge. Batgirl was strong, but Jackson was big, and when he fell, he took her with him.

The world spun around her as she plummeted. It was a thirty-story drop to the hard marble courtyard below. Instinctively, her hand went for her Utility Belt, but she'd used her grappling hook to save Felix back at the belltower.

Batgirl was in a free fall. She opened her arms, spreading her cape into glide mode, but she didn't have any forward momentum to take to the air. Her cape caught enough wind to slow her fall. She landed with a hard crack on the ground. Batgirl felt a painful pop as her shoulder dislocated, but she was alive.

By some miracle of luck, Jackson's belt had caught on the Wayne Library's rooftop gutter drain. But the boy was still unconscious, and thirty stories below him, all Batgirl could do was watch as the gutter gave way with a wrench and a tear.

Jackson fell.

"No!" she cried.

Just then came a flapping of wings. Something large and dark swooped down and grabbed Jackson right before his body hit the ground.

Batgirl's first thought was that Batman had arrived, but then she got a better look.

The creature that had saved Jackson's life was far larger than the beast the boy had become. An older monster. Stronger.

Kirk Langstrom, *the* Man-Bat.

Batgirl held her breath as the creature gently laid the boy down on the hard ground. It was so much bigger than she'd imagined. Massive. And she was in no condition for a fight.

Man-Bat leaned close and sniffed the unconscious boy, its labored breath echoing in cavernous lungs. As it passed its muzzled face over Jackson's body, its gaze came to rest on the empty syringe still stuck into the boy's arm.

Man-Bat let out a sound like a low whine. For a moment, Batgirl locked eyes with the creature.

There was no humanity in those red eyes, nothing of Dr. Langstrom that she could see.

But there was sadness. Bottomless, all-consuming sadness.

Then Man-Bat stood, and, with a terrifying screech, took flight. Batgirl watched until the flapping shape disappeared into the night sky.

"Oh, Doctor," said Batgirl. "I'm so sorry."

Barbara spent a week in the hospital, and she never returned to Gotham Academy. On the day she was discharged, a limousine arrived to pick her up.

"Good to see you, Alfred," she said as the tall butler held the door open for her.

"Good to see you, too, miss," he answered with a warm smile, "and in one piece."

Batman was waiting in the Batcave for her. He glanced at her arm, wrapped in a sling. "Glad to see you're safe."

"No more school," she told Batman. "I'd rather clean out Cobblepot's penguin cages."

Batman's mouth turned up in a grim grin.

"Also, I think I might be done with Batgirl, Bruce. For a while, at least."

Batman studied her for a moment. "You should take a break. Rest and recover. But what happened to Kirk Langstrom isn't your fault. It's his."

Barbara sighed. "It's terrible. He was so close to curing himself!"

"And he'll come close again. And next time maybe he'll succeed. But you did good work. You saved lives, and you saved Jackson Cobblepot from becoming a monster."

Barbara rolled her eyes. "He was already a jerk. Not sure that would have been any big loss."

"Felix Maroni has been expelled from for breaking into Langstrom's lab," said Batman.

"What about Nell? I know she screwed up, but her heart's in the right place, Bruce."

Batman paused before answering. "I was hoping you had more info on her. Has she reached out to you at all?"

"Me? No. Why?"

"Because she's gone missing. Nell Binder disappeared the same night you fought Man-Bat. No one's heard from her since. . . ."

Well, it's getting late. But I wouldn't
want you to go without finishing the tour.
Ah, this next fellow has a good story. And it's
short, sweet, and deadly.
I give you the ultimate fanboy—Jervis Tetch.
A man so obsessed with his favorite book that he
took on the persona of one of its strangest
characters—the Mad Hatter!

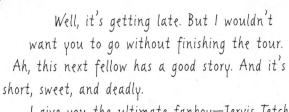

BINDER, NELL

FOUR

THE REAL ME

"Beware the Jabberwock, my son!
The jaws that bite, the claws that catch!
Beware the Jubjub bird, and shun
The frumious Bandersnatch!"

—Jabberwocky, a poem by Lewis Carroll featured in Through
the Looking-Glass and What Alice Found There

The Bat-Signal is a potent symbol. When Gotham City's average citizen sees the bat-shaped spotlight shining from the roof of the Gotham City Police Department, they know that their Dark Knight is watching over them. To them it means *hope* for a safer tomorrow.

But for the city's criminal underworld, the Bat-Signal means *fear.* Quite frankly, it's the only reason Batman tolerated such a public and showy means of communication.

But a man who dresses as a bat has a healthy respect for symbols, and so on this particular night, as he saw the glowing bat calling him from above the GCPD building, he answered. What he found, however, was something unexpected.

Instead of Commissioner Gordon, a small, weaselly man waited for him. He wore a green suit cut in a fashion straight out of the 1800s. A garish, polka-dot tie hung disheveled around his neck. And he was pacing back and forth, wringing his hands nervously and mumbling something under his breath.

The Caped Crusader stepped out of the shadows. "Jervis Tetch."

The little man shrieked at the sudden mention of his name and tripped over himself, landing on his back in a rain puddle.

"Batman! Oh, thank goodness!"

Jervis Tetch was a eccentric genius who had become obsessed with the book *Alice's Adventures in Wonderland*. He was so obsessed that he adopted the one of the book's more colorful characters from the famous tea party scene and began a life of crime. Like so many of the villains in Batman's Rogues Gallery, Tetch's genius could have been used to help people, but instead he devised crimes around the works of Lewis Carroll, author of his favorite book. Hypnotic hats that allowed him to use mind control on his victims were the latest of his inventions. Batman and Tetch had tangled many times, along with similarly themed accomplices who looked like they'd come straight from a children's story.

Tetch had even once forced Batman to fight a mind-controlled monkey. But tonight Tetch was alone. What's more, he looked genuinely desperate and afraid. Terribly, terribly afraid.

"What are you up to, Jervis?" said Batman,

using the Mad Hatter's proper name. "Where's Gordon? If you've hurt him . . ."

"No! No, I haven't hurt anyone, I swear!" Tetch looked nervously over his shoulder. "I've only come here for help. I . . . I don't know who else to turn to."

It was hard to know if Jervis was lying, as his state of panic meant that all the telltale signs of falsehood—increased heartbeat, and anxious, sweating, glances—were useless. But it was very unlike him to face Batman one-on-one. On top of a building full of cops, no less.

"Is someone after you?"

The Hatter's eyes grew wide. "Not someone, Batman. Some*thing*!"

Batman studied the villain, then said, "Talk. But know that one way or another, tonight ends with you behind bars. Even if I help you, you are still a wanted man."

Jervis nodded vigorously. "I'll tell you, but we must be quick! The beast will be here soon."

"What beast?"

For a moment, Tetch's mouth moved, but no sound came out. Like a word too horrible to name was stuck in his throat. He tried again.

"The beast that's after me, Batman, is . . . the Jabberwock!"

He began his story.

"It all started this evening, Batman. I was in my haberdasher's workshop, celebrating a rather brilliant victory my Wonderland Gang had scored against a chief rival of mine, and thorn in both of our sides, The Scarecrow. This wasn't the usual criminal turf war—oh no, this was about the Black-fire Pendant!

"I know you are something of an authority on the occult, Batman, so surely you've heard of it? It has the power to manifest your greatest dreams! I'd been searching for it for years, and finally tracked down a shady relic hunter who claimed to have found it.

"And wouldn't you know it, on the night I was to finally hold the Blackfire Pendant in my hands, The Scarecrow tried to steal it away. But that spindly stack of straw is no match for the Mad Hatter! I sent him and his boys running, retrieved the pendant, then returned to my haberdashery.

"I can tell from that look, Batman, that you think me a fool for believing in such magical power. Well, perhaps I am a fool, but not for believing. I am a fool for underestimating the pendant's power. It is a monkey's paw, Batman! A horrid object that now has me under its abominable curse!

"It all began that night, as I sat in my chair gazing into the jeweled pendant. Have you ever noticed, Batman, how fractured your reflection becomes when gazing into a jewel? It enchanted me, but it alarmed me at the same time.

"The cry of some kind of bird roused me from

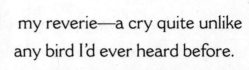

my reverie—a cry quite unlike any bird I'd ever heard before.

"This was then followed by another, even more peculiar sound: *Click-clack. Click-clack.* Like the tapping of a teacup against a brick wall, or a claw . . .

"At first, I thought someone was scratching at my door, perhaps my old friend the Dormouse had roused himself from slumber to join me for tea. But then I distinctly heard it again, and this time I divined the source of the peculiar sound to be just outside my window.

"My window!

"Pardon me while I pause to catch my breath, Batman, but the memory is almost as powerful as the image that I saw there behind the glass. I rose from my chair and gazed out the window. There, by the light of a feeble streetlamp, I saw . . . a beast. Twice as tall as a man, it stood on two legs as thick as tree trunks. Wings grew from its back—and oh, its eyes . . . its eyes burned like flames!

"The sound I'd heard was the sound of its claws, longer than daggers, impatiently tapping on the cement street.

"You see, it was waiting for me, Batman! Just as I knew it always had been! The Jabberwock!

"Aha! I can tell from your look that you think me mad. Mad as a hatter, no less! But I have always known that one day it would come for me.

"I am not as mad as I look, Batman. In fact, much of my life of crime has been one vast LARP—a live-action role-play based upon the world's greatest novel. I just like to *pretend*, that's all. Add in a little mind control, some extortion, and bank-robbing, and it was all good *literary* fun.

"But the Jabberwock . . .

"I was just a wee boy the first time I read Lewis Carrol's terrifying poem *Jabberwocky*. I was already obsessed with *Alice's Adventures in Wonderland*, and I'd finally convinced my parents—who did not understand the importance of books—to get me a copy of the sequel, called *Through the Looking-Glass and What Alice Found There*. Though it lacked a scene as compelling as the Mad Hatter's tea party, there was still plenty to delight in—the White Knight, the Gryphon, and the Mock Turtle!

"But then I came across . . . the poem. It was presented as a puzzle, one written in a way that

Alice needed to hold up to a mirror to read.

"*Jabberwocky.*

"It certainly sounded like nonsense, filled with made-up words like *brillig* and *gimble*, but being a bright lad, I got the meaning of it right away. This was the story of a *monster*. And it was accompanied by an illustration of the beast—terrifying, huge, and fearsome.

"I slammed the book shut then and there. And for many nights afterward, I'd lie in my bed imagining the call of the *Jubjub bird* just outside my window, warning me that the Jabberwock was near!

"Don't you see? It was the Blackfire Pendant. What dearer dream could I have than to see Wonderland brought to life? I would give anything to trade riddles with Cheshire Cat or sing songs with the Mock Turtle and the Walrus! But the pendant is slippery. In the same way a jewel distorts your reflection, the pendant distorted my dream. It made a bit of Wonderland real, all right. But it was the one part that terrified me. It brought to life the Jabberwock!

"The bird cry that I heard earlier tonight in my workshop *was* the Jubjub bird! Just as the poem says! Well, when I saw the beast outside my window, I took advantage of what little warning I had and I ran.

"I scooped up my very best hat and fled out the front door. In my haste, I fear I even left the Blackfire Pendant behind, though I am happy to be rid of it.

"The streets were dark, and for a moment I worried that I'd made myself more of a target by fleeing my hidden workshop. But then I heard the cracking and crashing of wood, and I knew that the Jabberwock had smashed its way inside my hideout. It was only by luck, and the cry of a lone Jubjub bird that I was still alive!

"But the monster was mere minutes behind me. There was no time to think, only to run!

"How far did I run, Batman? I don't even know. But eventually, the stitch in my side burned like fire and my heart, it beat so hard, I feared it would burst. I ducked into the nearest alleyway and paused to catch my breath.

"As I leaned against the brick wall of that dank Gotham City alleyway, I let the wet stone cool my feverish cheek. Was the beast still hunting me?

How long would this go on? Hours? Days? For-ever? *'The jaws that bite, the claws that catch!'*

"I'd certainly seen those jaws, the white teeth shining in the streetlight. I'd heard those claws tap-ping against the pavement.

"I could not run forever. I needed to make my stand!

"I collected myself. I straightened my tie and mopped the sweat from my brow. I had one mind-controlling hat—my only weapon. Perhaps if I could lure the beast close enough, I could hypnotize it.

"I'll confess, Batman, that I allowed myself a brief daydream of what it would be like to have the mighty Jabberwock under my control! The hypnotic circuitry should do the trick—I'd used it on beasts before.

"You remember the monkey?

"But to get close enough meant I'd be within reach of those claws that catch, the jaws that bite.

"In the poem, the mighty Jabberwock is killed by a knight, and I am no knight.

"*Click-clack. Click-clack.*

"There it was! Once again, I could hear the sound of claws against concrete. The light of a nearby streetlamp suddenly went out, casting the alley into darkness.

"So I waited and listened.

"I heard something move! The flapping of wings! Or was it the sound of my own heart beating in my ears?

"Peering into the dark, I stepped forward. If it was there, guarding the mouth of the alley, then I was trapped. No way out. No more running.

"The Mad Hatter would face his fear. Do battle with the beast!

"I steadied my hat, my *only* hat, and made ready. If the monster grabbed me, I might have a

split second before the jaws closed around me. I
would try to catch its gaze. I would try . . .

"Click-clack. Click-clack.

"The sound of its claws echoed through the
alley, but not from in front of me.

"Slowly I turned, hoping that all I would see
was a brick wall. But instead, I saw a gaping maw
filled with jagged teeth. I stared into eyes of *flame*.
The Jabberwock roared, and once again, I ran.

"I knew then that I could never fight the
Jabberwock. I've never been this afraid of anything in my entire life. I knew I needed a knight to
slay my dragon.

"I needed a Dark Knight!"

Jervis smiled at Batman with a mixture of hope
and extreme nervousness as he finished his story.
Well, most of it, anyway. Jervis had been forced
to hypnotize Commissioner Gordon into letting
him come up to the roof. Better to leave that part
out for now, though. Save it until *after* Batman

119

had slain the monster for him.

In fact, Jervis had the devious thought to order the mind-controlled Gordon to capture Batman and put *him* in jail! Wouldn't that be a fun turn of events? Yes, and he thought *Jervis* was the one who'd end up behind bars!

But *after* Batman killed the Jabberwock.

Jervis told himself to focus on the here and now. Jabberwock dead, Batman locked up. In that order.

"Ahem," said Jervis. "So, will you do it, Batman? Will you save me from the Jabberwock?"

Batman took a step forward and held up a penlight. "Let me see your eyes."

"What, you think I'm lying? I'm telling you the truth, Batman. I swear it on my hats!"

Jervis blinked away the spots as Batman shined the light into his eyes.

"I believe you," said Batman.

Jervis let out a long sigh of relief. "Oh, thank goodness. Now should we formulate a plan, or— say, do you own any swords?"

"I believe you are hallucinating, Hatter."

Jervis sputtered. "What? Didn't you listen to a thing I said?"

"Yes," said Batman. "And I listened when you told me that you'd done battle with The Scarecrow earlier tonight. Not long before you saw the Jabberwock, in fact."

"Regardless, I am being chased, Batman! Pursued!"

"Scarecrow's fear toxins cause vivid, terrifying hallucinations. A person with a fear of heights finds themselves atop an imaginary mountain ledge. An arachnophobe is terrorized by giant spiders. Jervis Tetch finds him chased by the fictional monster that terrified him when he was a child."

"No! I am in my right mind, Batman! It was the pendant's curse that set the beast on my trail, not some hack villain's fear gas!"

But the words had no sooner left Jervis's mouth than he spotted it, high in the sky.

Jervis pointed to the Bat-Signal above Gotham City. "There! You see it?"

A great winged beast flew in front of the spotlight and revealed itself—the Jabberwock had come!

"There, Batman, there!" cried Jervis. "Do you see it?"

But Batman didn't bother to look. "There's nothing up there but clouds."

"Well, *do* something!"

Batman put a hand on Jervis's shoulder and gave it a squeeze. "I am. I'm taking you in. Once the fear effects wear off, you'll be transferred to Arkham."

Confused, Jervis looked back at the sky. The Jabberwock was clearly visible now. Closer, and getting closer every second. It was right behind Batman now.

"It's behind you!" Jervis couldn't hold his ground a minute longer. He turned to run, and realized that Batman's hand was holding him in place with a grip like iron—it was almost clawlike!

"Let go!"

"Jervis, listen to me—"

Jervis fell to the ground and pulled himself rolled into a ball, covering his eyes and ears. How? How could this monster, this beast from Lewis Carroll's imagination, be real?

Unless . . .

Unless Jervis had had it wrong all this time. For years he'd adopted a persona as an homage to his favorite book. But he'd always known that it was a game. He was Jervis Tetch. Or so he'd thought.

If the Jabberwock was real, then so was the character *he* was playing! His eyes flew open with sheer joy! HA! He was really that character! But the joy lasted barely a second as he gazed upon the Jabberwock. Now that it was finally in the light, he could see its long ears and leathery wings. For the last time. Jervis Tetch giggled as the creature opened its fang-lined mouth, and—

Jervis Tetch opened his eyes. Batman was standing over him, but the sky above him was empty. They were alone on the roof together.

"Jervis, are you all right?" asked Batman.

"Jervis? Jervis is gone, Batman. The Jabberwock went and gobbled him up."

He let out a giggle like an amused child trying to keep a secret.

"What are you talking about, Jervis? Don't you know who you are?"

A crooked grin broke out over his face. "Oh, I know who I am. In fact, I've never been more sure! This world is full of mystery and danger, Batman. To survive it, you need to be as mad as a hatter. Which, luckily, now I am!"

The man once known as Jervis Tetch began to giggle again. A small sound at first, then on and on until he was hysterical with laughter.

He kept up the laughter all the way to his cell at Arkham. And for days, weeks, and months afterward, he told the story of the night Jervis Tetch disappeared to anyone who'd listen, and he became the person he was always meant to be.

On his way to the Batcave that night, Batman made a detour. He'd been unnervedbythewayJervis'smindhadfracturedright before his eyes. Jervis Tetch had always been an odd villain, but now he truly believed he was a character from the Lewis Carroll stories.

Perhaps The Scarecrow's fear toxin was to blame, as Batman had originally surmised, but now he had a nagging doubt.

Batman made his way to Jervis's workshop. Everything was as Jervis had described it—except the Blackfire Pendant was missing.

Batman was just about to leave when something caught his eye. He walked to the open window. There were gouges in the wooden sill there, each as long as a man's finger. Three deep gashes, like the claws of some great beast.

A giant bird, or . . . a Jabberwock?

On his way back to Wayne Manor, Batman made a call. "Alfred," he said. "I need you to look into the occult files. Give me everything you can find on the Blackfire Pendant. . . ."

Ah, poor Jervis. Scared into madness by something straight out of a children's story!

What's that? You don't like how that last one ended? Well, that is what we call a cliffhanger.

To get the truth about what became of Jervis Tetch's little magic jewel, you have to listen to one last story. It's here at the end of our tour. One last cell, an **empty** cell. Or is it?

Because that last cell holds a story that is far **worse** than anything we've dared to talk about tonight.

You'll feel fear like you've never known. . . .

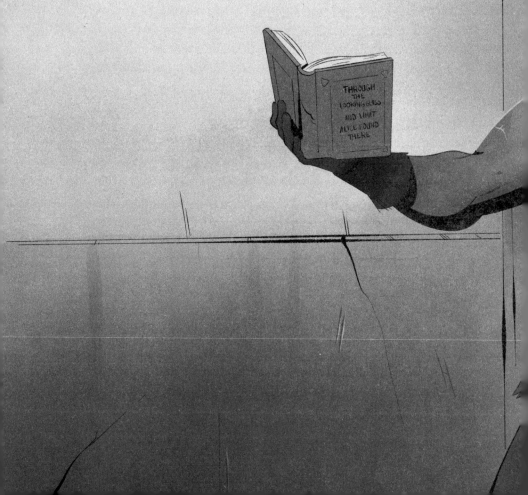

FIVE

SOMETHING TO FEAR

Dr. Jonathan Crane gazed into the multifaceted jewel pendant, and he didn't like what he saw. He'd never been a fan of his own face—too long by the standards of modern beauty, and a hawk nose. Watching his fractured features stare back at him now only compounded his displeasure. Dr. Crane's slender fingers found the burlap mask on his desk, and he pulled it on. Now when he looked at his reflection in the jewel, he saw jaggedly cut eyeholes and a stitched grin, the mask fastened at the neck with a loop of twine—like a hangman's noose.

His true face. The face of The Scarecrow.

What was it that Tetch had said about his precious jewel? That it made his dreams into reality? What a fool. Jervis Tetch had once been a man of science, like The Scarecrow, but he'd lost himself in a ridiculous children's story.

The Scarecrow was a scientist of *fear*. His life's work was the study of it on a biological level—the instantaneous chemical reactions stimulated by outside stimuli that could drive a person mad. The Scarecrow perfected fear in its weaponized form, a simple gas that triggered delusions drawn from a person's deepest horrors.

So, in a sense, the The Scarecrow was like Tetch's jewel. That made him smile. "I will make your dreams come true—only, they won't be good ones."

It was still a mystery why Jervis had suddenly abandoned his hideout; or why he'd gone shrieking into the streets. But when word got back to The Scarecrow, he'd been quick to act. He'd raided

Tetch's haberdashery with the hope of finding cash, or maybe even some of Jervis's admittedly rather brilliant hypnotizing technology. But to his surprise, he'd found the jewel, the famed Blackfire Pendant, lying there on the floor—the same jewel they'd fought over earlier that very evening.

The pendant would fetch The Scarecrow a small fortune on the black market. Superstitious fools would pay millions for it.

The Scarecrow pulled his gaze away from the jewel and looked out the window. The Bat-Signal lit up the sky tonight. That meant he would need to lie low. Time and time again, the Master of Fear had his plans foiled by Gotham City's Dark Knight. The Scarecrow glanced back at the jewel—could Batman ruin his plans to sell the pendant? After all he'd gone through, the thought of it ending up in the hands of that Caped Crusader made his normally cold blood boil.

Alas, not tonight. The jewel was his, but it would be best to get out of town for a while. Jervis Tetch's henchmen might want a little payback of their own.

And now with the Bat-Signal in the sky . . .

The Scarecrow would lie low until the heat died down. Yes, that was what he'd do. He had recently acquired a new base of operations, but it wasn't very secure. Up until recently, the warehouse at Pier 66 had belonged to the Ventriloquist. The rumors swirling around his latest arrest—ghosts and possessions, a haunted doll—made it the perfect fit for The Scarecrow and his gang. The Scarecrow was a sucker for a good ghost story. He'd moved in with his "ravens"—that was what he called the dim-witted henchmen who worked for him. A few of them complained about the raven masks, but The Scarecrow told them if they didn't like it, they could go work for The Joker. See how they liked robbing banks in clown shoes!

So, it was time to say an early goodbye to

their new home. The Scarecrow needed to pack his precious chemical lab and his reserves of fear gas. That was always tricky business, because one leaky canister could send his men into hysterics. Better tell one of the ravens to break out the gas masks. He holstered his fear-gas canister at his side and draped the jeweled pendant around his neck. Time to go.

But when he opened the door, the guards were not there. There were supposed to be two ravens stationed outside his door at all times—and no sleeping on duty! Tonight's shift should have been Knuckles and Bugsy. The Scarecrow had made the schedule himself.

"You can't get good help these days," he muttered. "Maybe a night in a locked room with a dose of fear gas will teach them."

The Scarecrow's lab was on the ground floor, and his office, or, as he preferred to call it, his *inner sanctum,* was on the fifth floor. So he walked down the long hall to the maintenance elevator. There would be ravens on each floor, and he could have just taken the stairs down one flight to find someone, but steps were harder than you might think for a man with a burlap sack mask over his head.

The elevator creaked and groaned as it arrived. When the cage doors opened, The Scarecrow rehearsed what he'd say to old Knuckles and Bugsy. But what he saw inside stopped him in his tracks. He'd found Knuckles and Bugsy, all right. They were tied up and unconscious, slumped back-to-back on the elevator floor.

A single bat-shaped boomerang was tucked into Bugsy's shirt pocket like a calling card.

"Batman!" shouted The Scarecrow, his shrill voice echoing through the warehouse. "Batman's here! Batman alert!"

No need to be subtle now.

But no one raised an alarm. The Scarecrow waited for the sound of footsteps running to his rescue, but all he heard was . . . silence. What if there *was* no one to raise an alarm? What if all his precious ravens had flown the coop? Or worse, what if Batman had gotten them all, like he had Knuckles and Bugsy?

"Scaaaaarecrooow."

The Scarecrow whirled around at the sound of

his name and drew his gas sprayer, ready to use it.

Batman was there, standing in the shadows at the end of the hall. The Scarecrow could see the distinct silhouette.

"Curse you, Batman!" cried The Scarecrow. He had found him. He *always* found him!

Batman said his name again, only instead of his usual throaty growl, his voice . . . gurgled and rasped. *"Scaaaaarecrooow."*

It didn't sound like Batman at all. Was this a trick? Some revenge of Jervis Tetch's? Whoever it was, they were about to experience their deepest fears. The Scarecrow fired his gas spray, filling up the hallway with the terror-tinged fog.

He waited for the horrified screams, but they never came. Instead, he heard . . . shuffling?

"Scaaaaarecrooow."

Batman emerged from the cloud of gas. His cape was ragged and torn and caked with mud. He looked like something from a horror movie. *Or worse yet,* thought The Scarecrow, *one of my own nightmares!*

"Scaaaaarecrooow."

The Scarecrow observed his own reaction

clinically. He was a man of science, after all. His heartbeat accelerated. He began to perspire heavily. His mouth tasted metallic, like copper, as adrenaline fueled his fight-or-flight response.

The villain backed into the elevator and hit the button to close the doors, while the shambling Batman continued coming closer and closer. The Scarecrow hit the button again. And again. But nothing happened.

Batman reached for him . . .

. . . and the doors finally shut. But they couldn't close all the way. Bony fingers wriggled at him through the door.

With a cry, The Scarecrow smashed his gas sprayer into the fingers, and they broke like dusty twigs. With a heave, the elevator began to move.

The Scarecrow allowed himself to take a breath, but the freight elevator was ponderously slow, and he squeezed himself up against the corner, as far away from the wriggling fingers as he could get.

Third floor . . .

Second . . .

First . . .

Suddenly, there was a heavy thump on the ceiling above him, like something had hit the roof of the elevator, followed by a dragging sound.

He's on the ceiling! He dropped down the elevator shaft!

The ground floor of the warehouse was a dark maze of crates that now stood between The Scarecrow and his freedom. Plenty of places within for Batman to attack him.

But what other choice did The Scarecrow have?

As he hurried though the warehouse, he listened for the slightest sound. He peeked around every corner. He'd made it more than halfway across, and still no bat.

No bat! And there, up ahead, was the exit! He could see the sign's dull red glow.

Then a shadow stepped out. The familiar bat cowl and cape blocked the light of the exit sign.

The Scarecrow fell to his knees. He was finished! Even in death, Batman had won.

"Get down and close your eyes." The Scarecrow obeyed.

Something flashed brightly, and The Scarecrow's vision turned red even though his eyes were shut tight, and a wave of heat struck his back.

"Scaaaaarecrooooooooooowwww."

He heard the gurgling call of his name, but it was behind him. Turning, The Scarecrow dared to open his eyes.

The batlike thing was standing there, mere feet away, the source of the blinding light. The flash burned brightly for a moment, then the batlike form disappeared in a cloud of smoke.

The Scarecrow couldn't breathe. He yanked off his burlap mask, but before he even had a chance to take in a full gulp of air, a gloved hand reached through the smoke and grabbed him.

The Scarecrow screamed. But then he felt an immediate wave of relief as he realized it was the hand of the real Batman.

Batman, alive and well. The Dark Knight examined some burnt remains while keeping a tight grip on The Scarecrow. "Magnesium flare," he said. "Only meant to blind it, but it went up like a torch. Interesting."

"Interesting?" cried The Scarecrow. "*Interesting?* You just burned up a walking corpse of yourself, and all you can say is *interesting*?"

Batman reached down and yanked the Blackfire Pendant from around The Scarecrow's neck. He was careful not to look directly at the jewel as he tucked it into a pouch on his belt. "I know the perfect place to keep this safe. I have a collection of . . . dangerous objects."

"I can't beat you even when you're dead!" The Scarecrow said with a moan.

EPILOGUE

And there you have it. Our final tale of horror—the tale of the fall of The Scarecrow at the hands of the Bat! Did he save me from that cursed jewel? Or did he just prolong my torment?

One man's fear is another man's favor. If you've learned anything tonight, it should be that fear is **deeply** personal. Unique. An art.

And my fear . . .

. . . my fear is **Batman**. I know that now. And as long as he is out there, I think I'll stay in here, where it's nice and safe. With all my friends.

I'll even save a cell for you here in Arkham!

Home, sweet home.

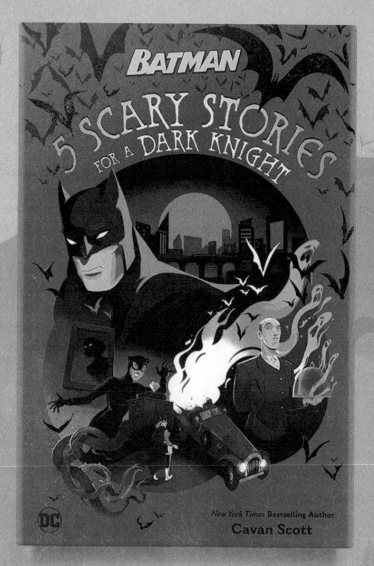

BATMAN

DARE TO DISCOVER
MORE SCARY STORIES WITH THE
DARK KNIGHT!